For Mat, whose hugs are always enough for two with a little left over ~ B.T.

For all the tiny kids, small kids, and the "BIG" kids at the BS3 Community Preschool. Thank you for all your help ~ S.J.

tiger tales
5 River Road, Suite 128, Wilton, CT 06897
Published in the United States 2020
Originally published in Great Britain 2020
by Little Tiger Press Ltd.
Text by Barry Timms
Text copyright © 2020 Little Tiger Press Ltd.
Illustrations copyright © 2020 Sean Julian
ISBN-13: 978-1-68010-190-4
ISBN-10: 1-68010-190-0
Printed in China
LTP/1400/2942/0919
All rights reserved
10 9 8 7 6 5 4 3 2 1

For more insight and activities,
visit us at www.tigertalesbooks.com

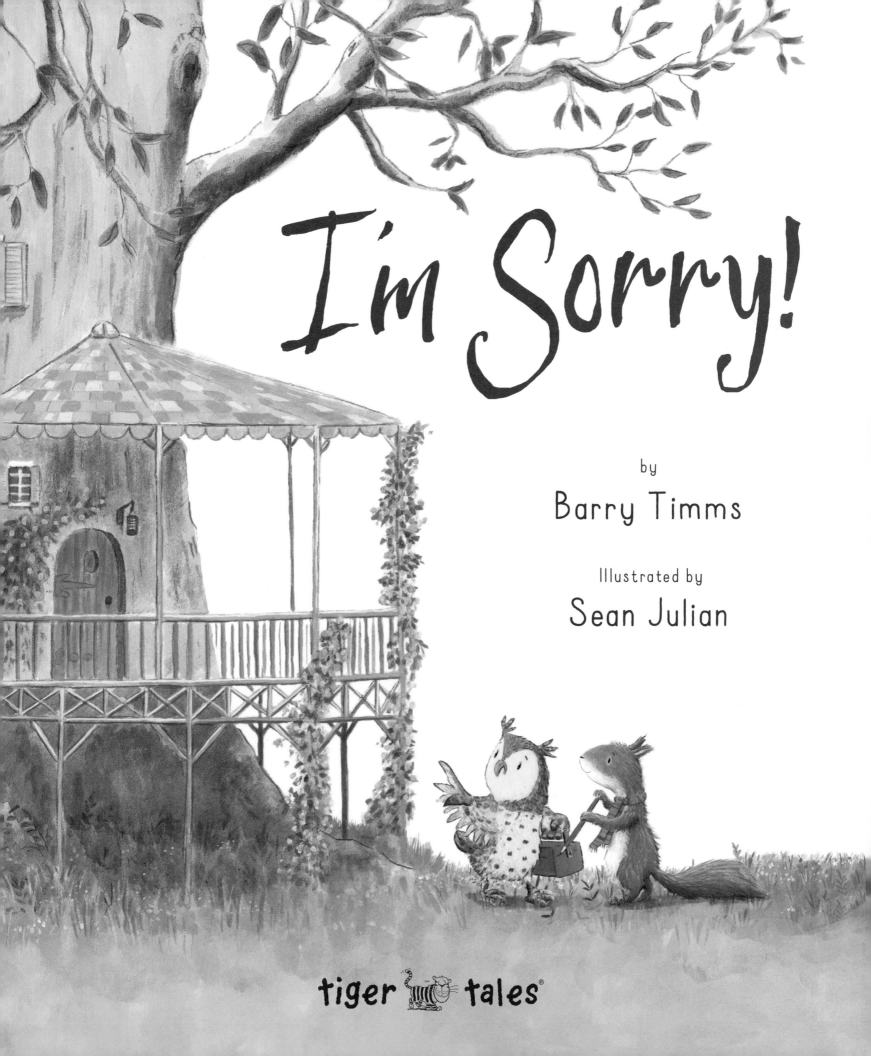

I'm Sorry!

by

Barry Timms

Illustrated by

Sean Julian

tiger tales

Every morning, Scribble and Swoop
met halfway at the bend in the river.

There never were two greater
friends in all of Walnut Woods.

Scribble always brought his special pencil.
"It helps me find the right words for my plays,"
he said. And when each play was written,
he called to Swoop, and the show began.

Swoop laughed and cried and
cheered for more.

Swoop also had her own special thing—a box
that never left her side. Tucked beneath its lid
were tools and screws and scraps of wood.

"Everything an owl needs to make stuff," she smiled.
There was **nothing** she could not build.

But Scribble and Swoop walked far each
day to meet at the bend in the river.
"Why don't we find a home we can
share?" asked Scribble one morning.

Swoop knew just the place.

There was room for two with a little left over.
"The perfect home for two best friends,"
said Swoop with a happy hoot.

After everything was unpacked, they sat in the shade of their beautiful porch. The breeze whispered. The bees bumbled. And that's when Scribble had a great idea!

This is the ideal place to perform my plays! he thought. *A theater!*

But Swoop was lost in
her own thoughts.

Plenty of daylight, and room for my tools!
A workshop, just for me!

Even best friends don't always think alike.

The very next day, Scribble woke up early and scurried over to the porch. "The world's greatest theater!" he announced, hoisting up the curtains.

He didn't see Swoop shuffle in with her special box of tools.

There was a HOOT!
a RIP!
and a CLATTER-BANG-CRASH!

Even the bees stopped bumbling.

The two friends glared.
"Get that stuff off my stage!" shouted Scribble.

"Your stage? Since when?" scoffed
Swoop. "This porch is MINE!"
"No—MINE!" Scribble snapped.

Then, grumbling and muttering,
they both marched off.

Swoop had never felt so furious.
She gathered Scribble's tattered curtains and
fixed them with big, angry stitches.

"All done!" she huffed and flung them
over a branch. Then she called to Scribble.
"Do your plays over HERE," she hissed,
"and NOT on my porch!"

But Swoop started to feel a little sad.
No amount of stitches could fix
her friend's hurt feelings.

The hours passed. The bees bumbled.
And all the while, Scribble fumed.

"Swoop has never been this rude!" he growled.
But already he missed his friend.

Scribble picked up his special pencil.
Time after time, it had helped him find the perfect
words and made problems disappear. But what words
could ever make things right between them?

And then Scribble found it!
The perfect word!

"I'll fix this once and for all," he declared.

Scribble stomped up to Swoop, took a huge breath, and yelled:

"SOR

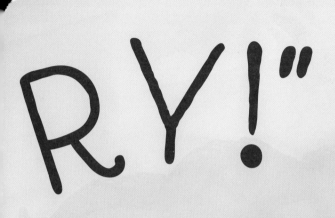

RY!"

But "sorry" is not a magic word.
It only works if you mean it.

"You're **not sorry at all!**" replied Swoop.
And it was true—he wasn't.

The word hadn't worked,
and now Scribble was
more upset than ever.

"**This pencil is useless!**"
he cried, and snapped
it in two.

All at once, he realized what he had done.
Then came a sob that shook him
from whiskers to tail.

Swoop's heart slumped with sadness.
"Scribble, I'm sorry!" she whispered. "The porch
wasn't mine to take. I ruined your curtains,
and I hurt your feelings."

"But I've been just as mean!" wailed Scribble.
"I never asked if I could build a theater."

Then Swoop took a step toward her friend . . .

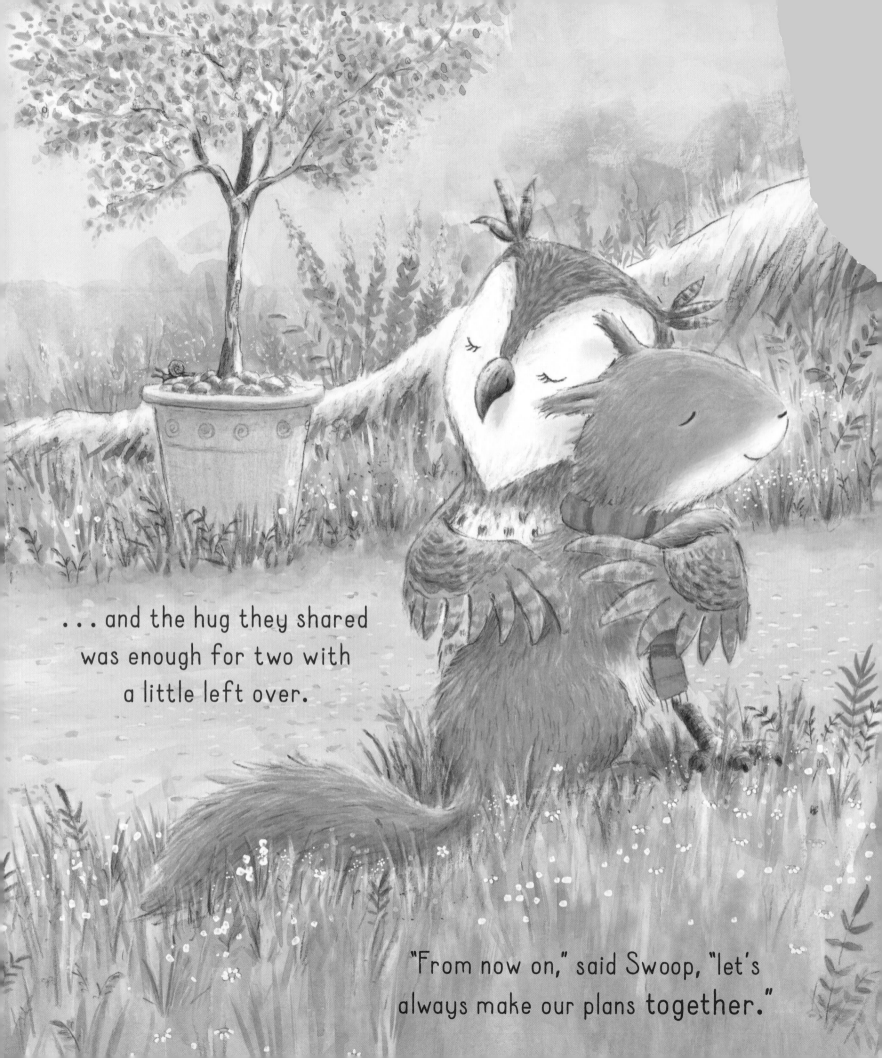

. . . and the hug they shared was enough for two with a little left over.

"From now on," said Swoop, "let's always make our plans together."

So Scribble picked up the tools and screws
and every last scrap of wood.

And Swoop fixed Scribble's pencil so that
the angry snap was just a memory.

Scribble and Swoop always remembered
that "I'm sorry" only works if you mean it.
And as for the porch, they agreed
to share it—

A place for writing in the morning, and
a place for making things in the afternoon.
And every evening, when the sun went down,
it was a theater for two best friends.